Grace's DANCE DISASTER

SaMaNTHa TURNBULL

ILLUSTRaTED by
SaRaH DaVIS

ALLEN&UNWIN
SYDNEY • MELBOURNE • AUCKLAND • LONDON

First published in 2015

Allen & Unwin
83 Alexander Street
Crows Nest NSW 2065
Australia
Phone: (61 2) 8425 0100
Email: info@allenandunwin.com
Web: www.allenandunwin.com

A Cataloguing-in-Publication entry is available from the
National Library of Australia
www.trove.nla.gov.au

ISBN 978 174331 986 4

Cover and text design by Vida & Luke Kelly
Set in 13pt Fairfield LT Std, Light
This book was printed in October 2017 by SOS Print + Media Group,
63-65 Burrows Road, Alexandria, NSW 2015, Australia

10 9 8 7 6 5 4

For Katie, Norman, Marie and Don

CHAPTER ONE

A fluorescent green string of snot is dangling from Chloe's nose like a pendulum. She has never looked prouder.

'That is seriously disgusting, sis' says her brother, Alex. 'Get a tissue.'

He's right. I have a strong stomach when it comes to gross stuff, but even I'm feeling a little queasy looking at Chloe's nasal mucus.

Chloe pokes out her tongue and shakes her head so the stretchy tendril wobbles a little more.

'*Kala myxa*, Chloe,' her grandmother chuckles. 'The best this week.'

'*Myxa*?' I ask.

Chloe translates Yiayia's Greek. 'Nice slime.'

Alex is almost choking on his toast. 'Yiayia! How could you encourage something so sick?'

'Relax,' Yiayia says. 'Would I be laughing if it was real?'

Chloe pinches the string between her thumb and forefinger and pulls it from her nose. 'Behold, my latest creation,' she says, swinging it above her head like a lasso. 'Snot made from water, gelatine, golden syrup and a touch of green food colouring.'

Alex snatches the specimen from his sister and throws it at the wall. It sticks and slowly slides down to the floor. 'You had me going there,' he says. 'Good one, Chloe.'

Trust Chloe Karalis to cook up a batch of fake snot for fun. She's a science whiz – who also happens to be one of my three best friends.

I'm Grace Bennett. I've stopped in at Chloe's on my way to athletics practice.

Alex is home from boarding school for the holidays. Next week he'll be starting his final year of school ever. I can't imagine being so old. Chloe and I will be going into fifth grade. We're ten.

'Would you like a cup of tea, Grace?' Yiayia asks.

I check my watch. Half past four. 'I better not, Yiayia. My mum is going to pick me up any minute.'

Yiayia places cups of chamomile tea in front of Chloe and Alex and kisses the tops of their heads. 'I miss you when you're at school, Alex,' she says. 'Your sister does too.'

Chloe has re-attached the snot to her nostril.

Alex sips his tea, peering over the top of the cup. 'Ah, my precious sister,' he says. 'What a delicate little flower you are.'

He's being sarcastic. Chloe and I, and our two best friends Emily Martin and Bella Singh, are more like tough cacti than delicate flowers.

The four of us are anti-princesses. Officially.

Last year we formed the Anti-Princess Club. It's for girls who are sick of being treated like princesses…or delicate flowers. None of us understand why anyone would want to be Sleeping Beauty or Cinderella instead of Aladdin or Peter Pan. That's the problem with fairytales – the girls are always so boring and helpless. We anti-princesses call them *unfairy*tales.

Beep, beep, beep. Beep. Beep.

'That's Mum,' I say. 'Thanks for having me.'

Thwack. As I stand up to leave, Chloe's snot hits me in the forehead. She grabs her ribs and bends over, heaving with giggles.

'Chloe, why did you do that?' Alex asks. 'Apologise to Grace.'

I roll my eyes. Alex still hasn't learnt the anti-princess motto: We Don't Need Rescuing.

I pry the slime from my face and roll it into a ball between my palms. 'Good shot, Chloe,' I say. 'Or should I say good snot?'

As I hug my friend goodbye I slyly slip the green ball into her cup of tea and wink at Alex.

CHAPTER TWO

ANTI-PRINCESS CLUB MATHS CHAT

MEMBERS ONLINE: 27   **MODERATOR:** Emily Martin

👤 Emily is online

EMILY: Hi everyone! Ready for the new school year?

AISHA: Hi Emily, I'm going into third grade – I'm really scared of Roman numerals – can you help?

ALLEGRA: Oh, me too.

EMILY: Trust me, you'll catch on quickly. The first thing you need to know is that to make Roman numerals, we use seven letters from the alphabet: I, V, X, L, C, D and M.

AISHA: Sounds confusing.

ALLEGRA: How can you use just seven letters for all the numbers in the universe? I don't get it.

EMILY: Hang ten, guys, I've got a visitor.

🔵 Emily is offline.

Emily and I are sitting in her bedroom chatting to some of the other Anti-Princess Club members.

When we first started the club, it was just us four best friends: Emily, Chloe, Bella and me. But as word got out, hundreds of other girls from around the country wanted to join. And the numbers just keep climbing.

We weren't sure how to wrangle such a big group at first. Our headquarters is an amazing treehouse in Bella's backyard, but even that wouldn't fit four hundred potential anti-princesses.

So Emily, being the club president as well as a mathematician and computer genius, built a website where everyone can meet in the virtual world. She moderates a chatroom set up specifically to help anti-princesses with their maths homework.

'Looks like there are a couple of girls freaking out about third-grade maths,' I say. 'Shouldn't they be enjoying their last few days of holiday time?'

Emily flips the laptop screen closed. 'They're just worrywarts,' she says. 'They'll be fine. Especially if they get a good teacher.'

I wonder who our new teacher will be.

Chloe, Emily, Bella and I had Ms Bayliss as our fourth-grade teacher. I think she secretly loved us anti-princesses, but teachers can't appear to have favourites.

'I hope we get someone as nice as Ms Bayliss,' I say. 'But not Miss Shapiro. I hear she's not into sport.'

Emily scratches her chin. She does that when she's thinking. 'Hmmm, well, that leaves Mr Ashton and Mrs Hughes for fifth-grade teachers,' she says. 'And I'd prefer Mrs Hughes, because she runs the computer club.'

There's a knock on the door.

'Come in,' Emily says.

Her dad's head pops through the doorway.

'Hi, Mr Martin,' I say. 'Welcome home.'

Emily's dad is a soldier in the Army. He's just arrived back from somewhere in the Middle East.

'Hi, Grace,' he says. 'I just wanted to check if you girls would like mattresses set up downstairs in front of the TV or if you'll be staying up here.'

I'm sleeping over at Emily's. It's always fun hanging with her family. Her mum is a little strange – she's a beautician with an at-home salon, AKA torture chamber – but her dad is easygoing, and her little sister, Ava, is super smart just like Emily.

'Maybe we'll sleep downstairs so we can watch some movies with Ava,' Emily says. 'Thanks, Dad, we'll be down soon.'

Emily's dad shuts the door and she flips her laptop open again.

AISHA: Emily? Please help!

ALLEGRA: Why do we have to learn Roman numerals if we don't live in Rome?

ZARA: What's a Roman numeral?

Emily is online.

EMILY: Calm down everyone. Let me talk you through it.

She shoos me away with one hand while typing with the other.

'Head downstairs and start watching the movie,' she says. 'It's *Cinderella*...just kidding! It's *Bend It Like Beckham* – an oldie but a goodie.'

I let out a little cheer and take one last look at Emily's screen. The frantic soon-to-be third-graders are typing pleas for help thick and fast.

'The teacher who gets those girls should be paying you,' I say. 'This is more than an online chatroom. It's an online classroom.'

CHaPTeR  THREE

Bella is bobbing in a sea of plastic drinking straws, oblivious to Chloe, Emily and me standing right behind her.

'Bats,' she mumbles.

I don't see any bats – the blood-sucking vampire kind *or* the cricket variety.

'Er, hello, Bella,' I say. 'We're all here.'

Bella jumps, and a pile of at least three hundred carefully arranged straws collapses on the grass around the ladder to the treehouse.

'Did you mean to say *drats*?' Emily asks. 'Because it looks like you're having a bit of trouble with whatever you're making here.'

Bella wipes her brow with her forearm as we kneel down to help her clean up the mess. 'No, I meant to say BATS,' she says. 'It stands for beams, arches, trusses and suspensions.'

An acronym. I should've known it was something to do with construction. Bella is a designer and builder. She loves anything artistic, but is especially good at creating complicated structures like the Anti-Princess Club headquarters.

'I'm working on a prototype for a bridge from the deck to the treehouse,' she says. 'But I just can't figure out what sort to build.'

Chloe, Emily and I all turn our heads at once to look at the back deck of Bella's house. We then look at the treehouse, then back at the deck. Treehouse, deck, treehouse, deck.

'You guys look like you're watching a tennis match,' Bella laughs. 'What's up?'

The treehouse is a long way from Bella's back deck. A bridge between the two would have to be enormous.

I don't doubt Bella's ability to build it, and her parents are so cool I bet they'd allow it. But, still, a bridge like that could take forever.

'How will you find the time?' I ask. 'And why? It's not as if you've got a huge river flowing through your backyard. We can easily walk across the grass to the treehouse.'

Bella sighs and dumps the last lot of straws in a bucket. 'You're right. I guess I've just been a little bored these holidays.'

She climbs the ladder to the treehouse and we all follow.

'I can't wait for fifth grade,' Bella continues. 'I need some cool projects to sink my teeth into. Speaking of sinking teeth into things, who wants a choccie?'

I grab a fistful of mini bars from the jar Bella

offers around. I'm always ravenous. I think it must have something to do with the fact I'm always exercising.

'What teacher do you want, Bella?' I ask through my mouthful of chocolate. 'And what about you, Chloe?'

They both shrug their shoulders.

'I'm not too bothered,' Bella says. 'But I'm worried about being put in a class alone.'

A glum feeling washes over us. The fifth grade is divided into four classes, and it doesn't take Emily's maths skills to figure out the odds of all four of us staying in the same class aren't great. We've been lucky to go through every year in the same room so far.

'Don't worry,' I say. 'We've been best friends since kindergarten, remember? Different class-rooms won't change that.'

Bella gulps down a piece of chocolate and nods. 'You're right. I need to build a bridge and get over it.'

I laugh so hard that I spit out a chunk of

brown chocolate mush. I point at it. 'It looks like poo!' I squeal.

The anti-princesses collapse with laughter. 'That's another reason we're such good buddies,' Bella says. 'We don't mind being a bit disgusting every now and then.'

CHAPTER FOUR

The trouble with having three brothers is that I'm always falling into the toilet.

For such a big family, it would really help to have a second bathroom, but our home is kind of cosy.

I pull myself out of the toilet bowl and flip down the seat. 'Can you pleeeeeeease remember to put the seat down?' I yell at no one in particular.

'Sorry, Grace,' Tom's voice calls back. 'Hope your bum's not too wet!'

I hear the other boys laughing in the distance. Tom is the oldest, he's thirteen.

Then there's me, ten going on eleven. Oliver is eight and Harry is six.

Mum knocks on the door as I'm washing my hands. 'Grace, can I come in? I've got something to show you.'

I honestly can't hide anywhere around here. No wonder I have so many sleepovers at the other anti-princesses' houses.

'Geez, Mum,' I say. 'Can you wait till I get out of the bathroom?'

'I'm sorry, Grace, but it's just too exciting to wait,' she says, opening the door. 'You're going to love this.'

Mum's holding an envelope. She pulls out a folded piece of paper. 'We got it in the mail today from the national soccer federation,' she says. 'I wanted to show you first.'

I scan over the first few lines.

We wish to give you advance notice of an upcoming match to be played at Newcastle City Stadium. The Newcastle Jets will play Manchester United on March 6 at 3pm.

A first round of ticket sales for selected VIPs will take place before remaining tickets are made available to the wider public.

I stop reading and jump up and down, almost slipping on the bathroom tiles. 'This is sooooo exciting! Dad can get the whole family tickets in that first round!'

Manchester United is the most famous soccer team in the world. I can hardly believe they're coming to my town. Tickets will sell out for sure.

Dad is a Very Important Person because he's one of the best junior coaches in Newcastle. Right now he's at a tournament on the other side of the state with some of his elite players.

Mum puts the letter back in the envelope. 'It can be a surprise for when he gets home,' she says. 'Unless he hears about it on the grapevine before then.'

I give Mum a hug. She's come a long way.

Mum and Dad were both raised in the country by old-fashioned parents. Dad actually grew up in the outback surrounded by boys. He'd barely met any girls before Mum.

So, until recently, Mum and Dad weren't too keen on me doing anything physical apart from ballet. They thought sweating wasn't ladylike, or something ridiculous. But once they found out that sport was my greatest love, they caved in and let me give up ballet so I could concentrate on athletics and soccer.

I guess it also helped when they saw me win every sprint in the Junior District Athletics Carnival. I was the fastest kid there – boy or girl. I don't mean to sound like a bragger when I say that. It's just a fact.

Tom appears in the bathroom doorway and Mum quickly hides the letter behind her back.

'What's going on in here, then?' he asks. 'Do you two like hanging around toilets?'

I roll my eyes.

'It's just…just girls' stuff,' Mum says. 'Move along.'

Tom looks scared by the prospect of 'girls'

stuff' and jogs down the hallway. The front door slams and the sound of his footsteps trails off outside.

'I want to keep it a secret from the boys until your dad gets home,' Mum says. 'It'll be a nice surprise for everyone.'

I link pinky fingers with her to promise I won't blab.

Well, I won't blab to my brothers, but I may just have to send an email to the anti-princesses. It's too sensational to keep all to myself.

CHAPTER FIVE

Chloe twists her long black hair into a bun and pushes her glasses up the bridge of her nose.

She passes her hairbrush to me and I give my blonde fringe the once-over. I don't look in the mirror. That's the good thing about having short hair, it doesn't take much boring maintenance.

'Did you know that scientists can test hair to see what has been through someone's bloodstream?' Chloe asks. 'I might keep a few strands from that brush and run some tests myself.'

Bella has already braided her brown curls, so I offer the brush to Emily.

She doesn't take it. Instead, she flips her red mop upside down and piles it under a baseball cap. 'Don't tell Mum I did that. She'd expect ribbons and bows on the first day back, but I just can't be bothered.'

We're getting ready at Chloe's because it's walking distance from school. Her parents left early this morning to take Alex back to his dorm, so it's just us and Yiayia.

I hear the kettle whistle from the kitchen. 'Breakfast is ready,' Yiayia calls. 'An extra-special meal for the first day of school.'

A tray of honey-drenched pastries is waiting on the table. We dig in, and for a minute or two there's no sound but the occasional satisfied groan.

There are always plenty of delicious treats at Chloe's place. Her apartment is above her family's Greek restaurant. Chloe actually invents some of the recipes they use. She says mixing ingredients can be similar to scientific experiments.

Chloe licks her fingers and collects our plates. 'We better head off,' she says. 'Don't want to be late on our first day.'

We all grab our backpacks and kiss Yiayia goodbye.

'*Kali tychi,*' Yiayia says. 'That means good luck. Not that you need it.'

As we hit the street, Chloe links arms with me. 'Are you nervous?' she asks. 'You know, now that it's actually happening.'

'I'm okay,' I say. 'It's like we were saying before. We'll all be okay, even if we are split up.'

CHAPTER SIX

Emily's eyeballs are moving from side to side as she counts the heads in the assembly hall.

'Just as I thought,' she says. 'There are 102 students. That will mean four classes.'

Four teachers climb the stairs to the stage. I recognise three of them as fifth-grade teachers from last year. The fourth, a broad-shouldered man in white sneakers, must be new.

The school principal, Mrs O'Neill, joins them. 'Welcome to fifth grade,' she says into the microphone. 'Let me introduce you to this year's teachers: Mr Ashton, Miss Shapiro, Mrs Hughes and Mr Talbot.'

They wave and we all clap.

'Mr Talbot has recently moved here from Greenville,' Mrs O'Neill continues. 'And as well as teaching, he will coach the school's soccer teams.'

Emily, Bella and Chloe shoot me a knowing look. I cross my fingers that I'm in Mr Talbot's class.

Mrs O'Neill puts her reading glasses on and pulls a clipboard from her briefcase. 'Could the following people please line up in the back left corner of the hall,' she says. 'You will be in Mrs Hughes's class this year. You may know her from the computer club.'

Emily takes a deep breath.

Mrs O'Neill reads out names in alphabetical order. 'Tao Liu, Jemima Long, Peter Lucas, Lisa McDonald, Keely Maris, Rose Menzies...'

Emily drops her bottom lip.

I give her a nudge. 'Hey, don't worry,' I whisper as Mrs Hughes leads her students out of the hall. 'This means we've got a better chance of being in a class together now.'

Miss Shapiro steps forward and I shudder. She's wearing stilettos – the least sporty shoe possible.

Mrs O'Neill starts calling out names again, and I close my eyes. 'Please not her, please not her,' I repeat under my breath.

I don't have to wait long. Bennett is close to the top of the roll.

'Gaynor Baxter, Lucien Beaumont, Philippa Bienke...'

'Phew.' I open my eyes. 'Two down, two to go.'

None of the other anti-princesses' names are read out for Miss Shapiro's class. We smile excitedly at one another. Maybe we *will* be grouped together again.

Mr Ashton gets up from his chair with a huff and a puff. He clasps his hands on top of his bulbous stomach. Something tells me he's not the sporty type either.

Mrs O'Neill gets through the Bs without calling my name, and I squeal a little. I've got

Mr Talbot, the soccer coach!

Mrs O'Neill ignores my noisiness and continues. 'Timothy Johnson, Madeline Jones, Chloe Karalis…'

Chloe's eyes widen. She's not sure whether she should be happy or upset. One thing's for sure – we're not in the same class.

We all hold hands as the rollcall continues. 'Lindsay McDonald, Jonah Mackenzie, Kobi Marshall, Fergus Nicholls…'

Emily practically tackles me in excitement. 'Woohoo!' she yells. 'We must be together, Grace!'

Mrs O'Neill pauses and looks in our direction. 'Calm down, girls. I still have a lot of names to get through, so please be courteous.'

She continues reading, 'Manu Rousseau, Sunny Ruskin, Dora Sarkis, Mabel Sedgwick, Bella Singh…'

Bella throws her arm around Chloe. At least they'll be together.

We zip our lips, but none of us care about the rest of the names. Bella and Chloe are in Mr Ashton's class and Emily and I are in Mr Talbot's. The anti-princesses have been divided, but none of us are alone.

'Fifty-fifty,' Emily whispers. 'It's a great result – and not just from a mathematical perspective.'

CHAPTER SEVEN

Our first morning back is whizzing by with choosing desks, getting-to-know-you games and the fresh scent of new notebooks. The usual stuff.

Mr Talbot tells us he loves all sports, but his favourite is soccer. I think we'll get along just fine.

'He seems okay,' Emily says as the recess bell rings. 'I wonder how Bella and Chloe are doing.'

Bella and Chloe's classroom is closer to the picnic tables than mine and Emily's. They're already eating their snacks when we arrive.

'Hello, hello,' I say. 'Have you two had a cruisy morning like we have?'

'We've been filling out surveys,' Bella says. 'Mr Ashton wanted to know our interests, strengths and weaknesses.'

I grab the edge of the table and do a few tricep dips. 'That would be easy for me. Interests: sport. Strengths: sport. Weaknesses: sitting still.'

Bella laughs. 'Well, I put design down as my main interest, art as a strength and concentrating as a weakness.'

Admitting to concentration problems is very honest of Bella. She has a tendency to drift into dreamland when she's in design mode.

'What did Mr Ashton say to that?' I ask.

Before Bella can answer, Mr Ashton himself appears from behind the computer labs. He must be on playground duty.

'Hello, girls,' he says. 'Which one of you is Bella?'

Chloe points at Bella, who smiles politely.

'Right, I have something for you,' Mr Ashton says. 'I think it's right up your alley.'

He pulls a rolled-up magazine from under his arm and hands it to Bella with an awkward smile. 'It was left in the staff lounge,' he adds. 'And I'd just read about your love of design in your survey, so I brought it straight out. See you back in class.'

'Thanks, Mr Ashton,' Bella says, unrolling the magazine.

As Mr Ashton heads off, Bella's jaw drops. She turns the cover outwards to face the rest of us.

Emily and Chloe gasp. I read the neon-pink masthead aloud. '*Pose*? What's that?'

'*Pose* is a spew-worthy fashion magazine,' Emily says. 'My mum has loads of them in her salon.'

Bella shoves the magazine in her backpack.

We all sit in silence for a moment.

Chloe tries to smooth things over. 'I guess Mr Ashton was just trying to be nice. He thought he was giving you something that you'd like.'

Bella glares at Chloe. 'Giving me a fashion magazine is like taking a vegetarian to a steak-house,' she says. 'It's like buying shoes for a snake. It's like giving a pet tarantula to an arachnophobe.'

Everyone nods. I can hardly think of a less appropriate gift for any of us. Except maybe a tiara.

'So what do we do?' Chloe asks.

'We educate him,' Bella says. 'Our new teacher has a lot to learn.'

I bet Mr Ashton didn't expect his first lesson of the year to be Anti-Princess Protocol 101.

CHAPTER EIGHT

'He's home!'

I can't figure out which brother yelled as all three of them run to the front door.

Tom, Oliver and Harry bowl Dad over as he stumbles through the doorway laden with soccer balls and suitcases.

'Mum!' I call out. 'Dad's back!' I join the boys in their tangle of arms and legs on the floor.

Dad pins me down and plants a kiss on my cheek. 'How was everyone's first day of school?' he asks. 'Come to the table and tell me all about it.'

The whole family moves into the kitchen where Mum is serving up fried chicken and vegetables – Dad's favourite. Dad puts his hands on Mum's hips and sniffs her hair. It's a weird thing he always seems to do when he gets home from a trip. 'Did you miss me?' he asks.

Mum playfully whacks him with a tea towel. 'Of course. You think it's easy looking after these four on my own?'

I take my seat excitedly. This is the moment I've been waiting for. Mum can finally reveal the news about Manchester United coming to Newcastle. Dad and the boys will flip out.

The boys start spewing out stories about school, soccer and other random, unimportant stuff.

I clear my throat. They ignore me.

'Erhem,' I try again. Still nothing.

'Mum has something to say!'

Mum smiles at me and grabs the envelope from a kitchen drawer. She waves it around in the air, not even bothering to pull the paper from the envelope. 'Manchester United are coming to Newcastle!' she yells. 'They're playing the Jets!'

Dad and all three boys jump up as though they've just won a million dollars.

'No way!' Tom says. 'Show us the letter.'

Mum passes the envelope to Dad. By the look on his face, he hasn't heard anything about the match while he was away. He speedily slips the paper out of the envelope and reads out loud. '*Dear Mr Bennett,* blah, blah, blah... *the Newcastle Jets will play Manchester United on March sixth...*'

Oliver bounces up and down like a hyper-active frog. 'It's true!' he screams.

Dad's eyes move from side to side as he continues reading to himself. Then his smile disappears.

'Honey?' Mum asks. 'What is it?'

Dad closes his eyes and inhales deeply. Something is definitely wrong.

'Dad?' I ask.

He looks at the letter again, then hands it to Harry.

Harry runs his index finger along each line until he finds where Dad was up to.

'A limited number of tickets will be made available for purchase by VIPs on February first before remaining tickets are made available to the wider public on February sixth.

'We predict both rounds to sell out quickly and strongly advise you to attend the box office in person on the day of the sales.'

Tom slaps himself in the forehead. Oliver slumps onto a chair.

'What?' Mum asks. 'What is it?'

I get a lump in my throat. 'We're too late, Mum,' I say. 'The VIP tickets went on sale today. We should have called Dad about the game yesterday so he could arrange for you to get in line early this morning.'

Mum drops the tea towel and covers her mouth with both hands.

I'm torn between feeling angry at her,

furious at myself and sad for Dad and my brothers. 'It's my fault, Mum,' I say, putting my arms around her. 'I didn't take proper notice of the sale dates on the letter, and I was too caught up in the first day of school today.'

Mum starts to sob. A tear escapes down my right cheek and I wipe it away with my sleeve.

'Now, now,' Dad says. 'The day's not over yet.' He takes the telephone from the wall.

'Please, please, please,' Oliver whispers. 'Please let there be some tickets left.'

We don't make a sound as Dad speaks to the person on the end of the line. 'Coach Bennett here. I'm calling to enquire about the VIP tickets to the Manchester United game …Yes, I received a letter…I am aware of the date…No…Right…Okay, thank you.'

Dad turns off the phone.

Mum gulps. 'Well? Are there any tickets left?'

Dad's gaze doesn't lift from the floor. He shakes his head and walks out of the kitchen.

The boys all slink away to different corners of the house.

I sniffle as I pat Mum on the back. 'It's not the end of it,' I say. 'We'll get there.'

We must get tickets in the next round. The Bennetts will be in the stadium when Manchester United plays. We *have* to be.

CHAPTER NINE

Mr Ashton is whistling to himself as he writes some quiz questions on the whiteboard.

He has his back turned to us as we enter the classroom. We've all arrived early to give Bella moral support as she clears up the misunderstanding over the fashion magazine.

'Hello, Mr Ashton,' Bella says.

Mr Ashton screams and throws a white-board marker across the room. Luckily we all duck in time.

'Oh dear,' he says. 'Sorry, girls, you startled me. I'm not used to students arriving before the bell. I've been planning some exciting assignments based on the answers to your questionnaires.'

Chloe raises an eyebrow suspiciously.

'There were quite a few of you who listed science as an interest,' Mr Ashton says. 'So I've organised two science-based projects for a group of you – one project for the girls and one for the boys.'

Chloe frowns. 'Um, what exactly are the projects, Mr Ashton?'

He pulls a cardboard box out from beneath his desk. 'Take a look.'

'Wow, Mr Ashton,' Chloe says, her face lighting up as she and Bella peer into the box. 'Is that a rocket, and a bottle of some sort of fuel to make it fly?'

Mr Ashton laughs a deep, snorty chuckle that makes his belly wobble. 'No, silly. It's a rocket and a bottle of perfume.'

Chloe opens the bottle and has a sniff. 'It smells like toilet cleaner,' she says, screwing up her face. 'What's it for?'

Mr Ashton laughs again. 'It's *perfume*,' he repeats. 'You know, to make you smell pretty.'

Bella groans. She's figured it out. 'So, the girls get to make perfume. And the boys get to make rockets.'

Chloe's face reddens to a furious crimson, but Mr Ashton doesn't catch on.

'I went to the biggest toy shop in the city to do some research,' he says. 'And they had marvellous perfume-making kits in the girls' section and rocket-making kits in the boys' section. That's where I got the idea from.'

Bella grabs Chloe's shoulders. I'm not sure whether it's to restrain Chloe from throwing the perfume onto the floor in a fit of rage or to stop her from fainting in shock over their new teacher's ignorance. 'Take a moment, Chloe,' Bella whispers. 'Collect your thoughts.'

Mr Ashton is beaming as he opens a folder

and pulls out three pieces of paper. 'It's your lucky day too, Bella. Any ideas about your first big assignment?'

Bella gazes at the image Mr Ashton has handed her. I lean over and take a peek. It's a drawing of a woman in a white ball gown.

'Is it a…a *princess*?'

If Mr Ashton says yes, we may explode.

'Almost,' he laughs. 'It's a bride. There were three of you who listed design as a passion. The other students, Julie and Petra, said they were interested in fashion, so I assume that's what you meant too. I spoke to the other girls yesterday and Julie suggested you all design a wedding gown. I think it's a magnificent idea.'

Bella slowly scrunches the paper up in her fist.

Mr Ashton looks a little concerned, but then he grins. 'Ah, I understand. You're an artist and you want to design an original gown rather than copy a picture. Admirable, very admirable.'

The bell rings before Bella can even begin to explain how wrong he is.

Emily and I head for the door as Bella and Chloe turn to look after us with expressions of absolute despair.

I know we said we'd be cool if we were separated, but now I'm not so sure.

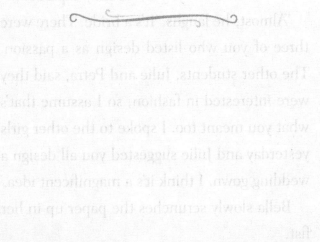

CHAPTER TEN

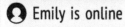

ANTI-PRINCESS CLUB MATHS CHAT

MEMBERS ONLINE: 43   **MODERATOR:** Emily Martin

👤 Emily is online

EMILY: Hello! How is everyone coping with their first week back at school?

MARISSA: Hi Emily! I am loving my fourth-grade teacher, Ms Bayliss.

ELISE: Hey Emily, how do you figure out the square root of something?

TESS: Hi Emily, what is a prime number?

Bella, Chloe and I are waiting patiently on the floor of the treehouse while Emily types so quickly her hands are a blur of movement. We're busting to start our next meeting of the Anti-Princess Club.

'I know you want to help everyone, Emily,' Bella says. 'But we're going to run out of time.'

> **EMILY:** Sorry guys, got a meeting to get to. I'll answer more questions later.

She stays logged on, but pushes the laptop away. 'I declare this meeting of the Anti-Princess Club in session,' she says. 'Let's get down to business.'

Chloe is the first to vent.

'I can't believe Mr Ashton,' she says. 'Can anyone tell me why he thinks girls and boys should be given different science projects? And why the boys get to do something cool like launch rockets, while the girls have to make lame, boring, smelly stuff that serves no purpose?'

I bend into a yoga pose I saw on TV once. Apparently it's effective for reducing stress. I'm not sure if it's helping my mind, but it's a good stretch for my quadriceps. 'Let's try to stay calm,' I say. 'Mr Ashton obviously needs help. He's stuck in the olden days when girls and boys were treated differently.'

Chloe nods. Her yiayia has spoken to us about what life used to be like for girls.

'And maybe he's used to the type of girls who, you know, actually wear perfume and stuff,' Emily says. 'There are people like that out there. My mum is one of them.'

Chloe stares up at the stars being projected onto the dome-shaped ceiling. 'I'd like to propose our first mission for the year,' she says. 'I will make the spew-worthy perfume, but I'll also build a rocket – to prove to Mr Ashton that girls can do *any* type of science project.'

Emily opens her computer and creates a new document.

Mission Blast-Off: Show Mr Ashton that girls can do any science project

'All in favour?' Emily asks.

We all raise our hands.

Oooooeeeeeee, ooooooeeee, ooooooooeeeee.

'It's the emergency signal!' Emily says.

Emily created a chatroom function that allows anti-princesses to get her attention if she's logged on but not responding. It's only supposed to be used in true emergencies – like someone's mum entering them in a beauty pageant.

We huddle around as Emily clicks on a flashing red flag in the corner of the screen.

RIHANNA: Emily, are you there? It says you're online. Hello? Hello?

EMILY: Yes, Rihanna, I just turned away from the laptop – what's the problem?

RIHANNA: I thought you should know that me, Sherri and Gemma got into trouble today for chatting on the Anti-Princess Club website.

EMILY: What do you mean? Your parents were angry?

RIHANNA: Not exactly...we were chatting at school. During class.

EMILY: Rihanna, this isn't exactly an emergency, is it?

RIHANNA: Well...Miss Shapiro demanded to see what website we were chatting on. She wrote down the web address and everything.

Emily stops typing and turns to us. 'What does that mean?' she asks. 'Do you think Miss Shapiro would have a problem with the site?'

I can't see why any teachers would be upset about the Anti-Princess Club website. After all, Emily is doing them a favour with all her online tutoring. 'She was probably just angry that Rihanna and the other girls weren't paying attention in class,' I say.

EMILY: Thanks for letting me know, Rihanna. From now on, just make sure you don't chat in class, OK?

RIHANNA: Sorry, Emily.

Emily is offline.

'Do you think we could get in trouble for this too?' I ask. 'You know, because it's our website.'

Emily closes her laptop. 'I've never been in serious trouble at school before,' she says. 'But I guess there's a first time for everything. And some of us aren't having much luck with teachers so far this year.'

CHAPTER ELEVEN

A Darth Vader look-alike is standing on my front lawn.

'Pick up these pipes for me, will you?' it says. 'You're the muscly one around here.'

It's Bella, in a welder's mask, gloves and leather jacket. She's even holding a small blowtorch. Half a dozen metal tubes are lying next to her feet.

I pile them into my arms. 'What are you up to, Bella?' I ask cheekily. 'Shouldn't you be designing a wedding dress or something?'

She points the torch in my direction. 'Watch yourself, Grace. I'm armed and dangerous.'

I follow her into my bedroom and dump the pipes on the floor.

Bella flips up her mask and cranes her neck to look at my ceiling. 'Just as I thought – the perfect spot.' She pulls a pair of black goggles from inside her jacket and throws them in my direction. 'Put these on.'

'For *what*?' I ask.

'Duh,' Bella says. 'To protect your eyes.'

I was actually asking what she meant by 'perfect spot', but I don't get time to clarify before Dad walks past and does a double-take. 'What the— Is that a *blowtorch*?'

Bella takes off her mask and sighs. 'I'm surprising Grace with a chin-up bar, Mr Bennett. I just need to weld a few pieces together and attach it to the ceiling.'

My own chin-up bar! What an awesome idea.

Dad storms in, shaking his head. 'No, no, no.' He holds out a hand for Bella's blowtorch.

'It's my welding gear, Mr Bennett,' she protests. 'I know what I'm doing.'

Dad takes the torch and turns a knob, which makes a hissing sound. Bella quickly snatches it back. 'Careful, Mr Bennett! That's gas. You could've caused some damage.'

'I need to check this with your parents, Bella,' Dad says. 'Don't light that thing until I call them, thank you very much. Then we'll discuss whether I'll let you use it in my house.'

Bella shrugs as Dad leaves the room. She's got nothing to hide. Her parents supply all her gear – everything from modelling clay to barbed wire.

I flop onto the bed. 'Sorry about this,' I say. 'I think he's extra grumpy since missing out on that first round of Manchester United tickets.'

'Hey, I read an article about one of the ManU players in that hideous *Pose* magazine,' Bella says. 'You know, the one Mr Ashton gave me?'

'How could I forget?' I say. 'But why was there was an article about soccer in a fashion magazine?'

Bella laughs. 'It wasn't exactly about soccer. It was an article about how one of the players is getting married in the first week of March. Boring.'

'Maybe they're getting married here in Newcastle,' I say. 'Their match against the Jets is March sixth.'

Bella mimes an over-the-top yawn to show her lack of interest in the wedding.

'Perhaps you *could* design the bridal gown, Bella,' I say. 'That would impress Mr Ashton –

you could be a designer to the stars!'

Bella points the blowtorch in my direction again. 'A gown is a gown, Grace. I won't be designing any such thing, so I suggest you pipe down.'

Dad returns at exactly the wrong time.

'Are you pointing that blowtorch at my daughter?' he yells. 'That's it! I couldn't reach your parents, so I'm sending you home myself. Out, Bella!'

We don't mean to be disrespectful, but Bella and I both start giggling. We know there's no use arguing with Dad.

'See you later, Grace,' Bella says. 'Chin up! Although that may be a little hard without a bar.'

CHAPTER TWELVE

Beep, beep, beep. Beep. Beep.

I smack the alarm clock and jolt into a sitting position. There's no way I'll be sneaking a few extra minutes of sleep today.

'You up, Grace?' Dad calls.

I throw down the doona and call back: 'Sure am!'

I can hear the shower running. It must be one of the boys. I don't want to hold everyone up, so I change out of my pyjamas and into a tracksuit without bothering to wash my face or brush my teeth.

Tom and Harry must have been thinking

the same thing, because they're sitting in the lounge room fully dressed, with mop-top bedheads.

'Oliver had better be quick,' Tom says. 'We need to get there as soon as we can.'

Dad packs a thermos and six bananas into a bag. 'Come on, Oliver! We're all ready.'

The shower stops running and Oliver calls, 'I'll just be a minute.'

Mum starts pacing the hall. I know she feels responsible for missing out on the first round of Manchester United tickets. I do too.

I follow her and gently touch her shoulder. 'Calm down, Mum,' I say. 'It's going to be okay.'

She looks at the grandfather clock. 'I don't know, Grace,' she says. 'Maybe we should've camped overnight.'

Tickets go on sale at nine this morning. We live half an hour from the box office. I'm sure there will be plenty of people lined up already, but we're giving ourselves more than enough time to guarantee a good spot.

Tom and Harry follow Dad out to the van. I'm about to do the same when a crash echoes down the hallway.

'*Aaaaaaahhhhhhh!*'

I run to the bathroom with Mum on my heels, yank the door open and see my half-dressed brother sprawled on the tiles.

'Oliver, what's the—'

Mum screams. Oliver's right foot is sticking out an awkward angle and his ankle has swollen to the size of an orange.

'Call an ambulance!' Mum yells.

I run back into the hallway and collide with Dad, who pushes past me and Mum into the bathroom. He takes one look at Oliver and starts ordering us around.

'I need an ice pack,' he says, and Mum rushes to the freezer. 'Grace, I'm going to lift Oliver up – I need you to hold his ankle and keep it elevated above the rest of his body.'

I slide my hands under my brother's ankle and lift until it's higher than his torso.

'There's no use calling an ambulance,' Dad says. 'We'll make it to the hospital quicker ourselves.'

Mum helps Dad lay Oliver down on the minivan's backseat and I prop his leg up on a pile of blankets. His eyes are squeezed tight, with tears running down his cheeks.

'It's going to be okay,' I tell him. 'We're taking you to the hospital.'

Mum climbs in the front as Dad starts the engine.

'What happened?' asks Tom.

I shake my head. 'I guess Oliver slipped. He was probably in too much of a rush.'

I catch Dad's worried reflection in the driver's side mirror. The minivan zooms through the neighbourhood, along a few back alleys and onto the freeway.

Oliver moans. His face has turned a ghostly shade of white.

'Nearly there, Oliver,' Mum says. 'You're doing so well.'

Dad mounts the kerb outside the emergency department and slides the minivan door open. Cradling Oliver like a baby, he dashes into the hospital with the rest of us behind him.

The nurse at the front desk gasps when she sees my brother's ankle. 'Straight through here,' she says, motioning behind some curtains.

Dad lays Oliver down on a bed and we all crowd around.

The nurse frowns. 'No, this won't do. The children will have to take a seat in the waiting room. There's not enough space in here.'

Tom and Harry are about to argue, but Mum puts a finger to her lips. 'You heard the nurse,' she says. 'We'll see you out there soon.'

I follow the boys into the waiting room and look at my watch.

Half past five. We won't be out of the hospital in time to snag the tickets.

CHAPTER THIRTEEN

'Please tell me that putrid odour didn't come from your butt, Chloe,' I say. 'It doesn't smell human.'

Bella laughs, then catches a whiff herself. 'Whoa. I need some air.'

Emily is the next to take a sniff. She gags and starts breathing heavily through her mouth.

Chloe pinches her nose too, and her voice goes all nasal. 'I'm afraid my body can't take credit for that,' she says. 'But I'm glad you find it so stinky.' She pulls a lidless jar out from underneath her bed.

'What is it?' I ask.

Chloe screws a lid on the jar, then seals it in a plastic bag. 'This, my friends, is an experimental brew for my perfume project,' she says. 'Otherwise known as rotten eggs whisked with vinegar. I think it's time to throw it out.'

Yiayia takes the bag. 'I think you will fail your first assignment, *paidi mou*,' she says.

'This is not a pretty fragrance. In the bin it goes.'

Chloe cackles like a witch. 'What is pretty, anyway?' she says. 'One person's roses could be another's rotten egg and vinegar.'

Yiayia shudders as she heads for the door with the 'perfume'. '*Nobody* would like to rub this behind their ears.'

Emily taps a pen on Chloe's desk to get our attention. 'I declare this meeting of the Anti-Princess Club open,' she says. 'Grace has already indicated she has an urgent matter of business, so let's start with her.'

She, Chloe and Bella all turn to me with sympathetic expressions. I emailed them when my family, minus Oliver, finally got home from hospital.

By the time we made it out of the emergency department the box office for Manchester United tickets was well and truly closed. They had sold out within an hour of the doors opening.

'As you know, we didn't get tickets to the big game,' I say. 'Oliver is going to be in hospital for a week or so. He has to keep his leg elevated for a few days so the swelling can go down enough for it to be operated on. Then he'll need therapy.'

Bella gives my knee a little pat. 'You're an awesome sister, Grace,' she says. 'Your whole family is awesome for putting Oliver first.'

There was never any question that Mum, Dad, Tom, Harry or I would leave the hospital to get those tickets. My brothers may test my patience sometimes, but I love them just as much as the anti-princesses.

'But the thing is, there's no more soccer-loving family in all of Newcastle than the Bennetts.' I grab my toes and pull them back towards my hips. Sitting still in hospital for more than six hours yesterday was not easy. 'So, I'd like to set another mission. I don't know how I'm going to do it, but I need tickets to that game.'

Chloe shifts uneasily in her seat. 'Mission Blast-Off will be easy. Getting tickets to a sold-out match is more like a dream.'

Chloe is right, but something in me thinks we can do it. I look to Bella and Emily for support.

'It *is* a dream,' Bella says. 'But dreams can come true.'

The decision rests with Emily. 'Okay, Grace,' she says. 'Mission ManU: Get Manchester United tickets for the Bennett family. All in favour?'

Bella, Emily and I raise our hands. Chloe hesitates, then sticks her arm in the air as well.

'We can figure out how we'll do it later,' she says. 'There must be a way.'

CHAPTER FOURTEEN

ANTI-PRINCESS CLUB MATHS CHAT

MEMBERS ONLINE: 47   **MODERATOR:** Emily Martin

🔵 Emily is online

EMILY: Whoa, 47 members online – that's a lot! Sorry if I can't get to all of you this morning, I only have ten minutes before class starts. Who wants to go first?

AISHA: Thank goodness you're here, Emily. Allegra is being a cow.

ALLEGRA: It's not me, Emily. Yesterday, Aisha had to choose a partner for a drama activity in class and she chose Lincoln. I mean, he's a boy, and I'M SUPPOSED TO BE HER BEST FRIEND!

AISHA: Why don't you tell her how you called me a loser?

EMILY: Hey, hey, settle down guys! This is supposed to be a chatroom for maths help, not playground dramas.

AISHA: But Emily,

EMILY: That's enough! Thanks for wasting my time, not to mention the other 44 people online who probably needed actual maths help.

🔘 Emily is offline

Emily slams her laptop shut. 'I don't understand some people, Grace,' she says. 'We weren't like that in third grade, were we?'

That's an easy question to answer. 'Certainly not,' I say. 'We've never had a major fight. Never will.'

Emily extends her pinky finger and I link it with mine. It seems like a big promise to make, but we're sure it won't be broken.

As we head down to the corridor towards our classroom an announcement comes over the loudspeaker. *'Could the following students report to the principal's office immediately: Emily Martin, Bella Singh, Grace Bennett and Chloe Karalis.'*

Startled, Emily and I stop in our tracks. None of us have ever been called to the principal's office.

A group of sixth-grade boys point at Emily and me. 'Ooooooooh,' they call. 'The anti-princesses are in trooooooouuuuuble.'

We start the walk of shame to Mrs O'Neill's

office. Chloe and Bella bump into us halfway there.

'What do you think it could be?' Bella asks.

'All of you, inside,' Mrs O'Neill interrupts. She's standing outside her office waiting for us, wearing a cat's-bum mouth.

We follow single-file into the principal's office. It's not what I expected. There are daisies in a vase, a gold-framed photo of a fluffy dog on her desk and a painting of a rainbow on the wall. Not scary at all.

'Take a seat,' Mrs O'Neill says.

There are only two chairs, so Bella and Chloe share one while Emily and I squeeze onto the other.

'I'm going to cut to the chase,' Mrs O'Neill says. 'I know you all call yourselves "anti-princesses", but who built the Anti-Princess Club website?'

Emily slowly raises her hand.

'Emily Martin, the computer whiz. I should've known.' Mrs O'Neill speaks as if she's just finished sucking on a lemon. 'And what role do the rest of you play?'

'Well…we're all in the Anti-Princess Club,' Bella says.

Mrs O'Neill shifts her gaze from us to her computer screen. The maths chatroom is up on the monitor, messages popping up every few seconds.

We all lean across her desk to take a closer look.

KARA: You're nothing but a dobber, Justine.

JUSTINE: Oh yeah? Well, I saw what you did to Kelly at basketball.

KELLY: Kara, you're just a jerk.

TAMMY: Watch your back, Kelly. How about the time you stole Aisha's seat and she was forced to sit up the back with Joey?

Emily's head is in her hands.

'It says you're the moderator, Emily,' Mrs O'Neill says. 'But how involved are the rest of you?'

None of us quite know what to say. Emily runs the chatroom, but we can't leave her to be punished alone.

'Well, I sometimes help Emily moderate,' I say.

Emily lifts her head. 'Nice try, Grace,' she says. 'It's just me, Mrs O'Neill. I'm the president of the Anti-Princess Club. I built the website and I run the chatroom.'

Mrs O'Neill peers over her glasses to study Emily's face, searching for any sign that Emily's lying. 'I find it very difficult to believe that a single ten-year-old is responsible for such a complicated operation,' she says. 'But I am also aware of your technical prowess.' She stands up and folds her arms. 'Last chance. You're telling me that you're the sole operator of this chatroom, Emily?'

I open my mouth to speak again, but Emily hisses: *'I don't need rescuing.'*

Mrs O'Neill hands Emily a red card. I'm not sure what it means in school terms, but

I do know it's the severest form of discipline you can be handed on the soccer field.

'We have a strict anti-bullying policy at this school as well as rules about appropriate use of technology,' she says. 'While I can't see any evidence of you engaging in bullying yourself, Emily, I'm afraid I have to hold you responsible as the creator of this online haven for gossip and nastiness. This card represents ten lunchtime detentions. Starting today.'

Emily looks at the card as if it's a death notice.

I slowly stand up and the other anti-princesses follow.

'One more thing, Miss Martin,' Mrs O'Neill says. 'I want that website taken down. ASAP.'

'But I can't—'

I gently push Emily out of the office mid-protest. Ten lunches without our president is enough punishment for now.

CHAPTER FIFTEEN

Anyone would think we've just been to a funeral. We're as sad as polar bears in the tropics, especially Emily.

'Ten detentions is one thing,' she says. 'But being ordered to pull down the website is disastrous. I worked so hard to build it – and I'll be abandoning all the other anti-princesses.'

I put my arm around her. 'It seems so unfair,' I say. 'Surely we could've just weeded out the bullies somehow.'

Emily shrugs my arm off her shoulders. 'No use arguing with Mrs O'Neill,' she says. 'I'm just glad we don't have to catch the bus today. I'm so depressed.'

Beep, beep, beep. Beep. Beep.

Bella's mum is across the road. She has a rare afternoon off and is picking us up.

'Turn those frowns upside down, sad sacks,' Dr Singh says as we climb into the car. 'I've got some popcorn, chocolate and a box of mangoes for your meeting this afternoon.'

Four half-hearted thank-yous emerge from our mouths.

'Okay, what's up?' Dr Singh asks. 'This is not like you girls at all.'

Bella turns on the radio. 'I'm sorry, Mum,' she says. 'We just need some time to dwell, then we'll tell you all about it. I promise.'

A country song about a man who stole some cows and went to jail hums through the speakers. It's very dreary. Quite appropriate, really. Then the music fades and a loud, over-the-top announcer comes on air. *'And, in breaking news, Manchester United players have arrived in our fair city to settle in before their match against* the Newcastle Jets. *We'll let you in on some of their pre-match plans after this ad break.'*

I squeal and almost jump out of my seat. Bella, Chloe and Emily smile for the first time in hours.

'That's more like it!' Dr Singh says.

The announcer's voice booms through the car again. *'If you're a soccer fanatic, pass by the Harbour View Hotel to catch a glimpse of the team. Our sources say that's where they'll be based while they're in Newcastle.'*

I squeal again.

'And in other ManU news, striker Daniel Hastie will be marrying his rock-climbing fiancée Svetlana Karpinskaia while they're here. They told reporters they're planning a small ceremony with no bridesmaids or groomsmen, but they're yet to decide on an exact location. Karpinskaia said they were scouring Newcastle for somewhere unconventional and unique. Now for our next hot hit on a hundred point nine, always on time, triple L FM.'

Bella turns the radio down. 'Did you hear that?' she asks.

Everyone nods excitedly.

'I mean, did you hear the bit about the wedding?' Bella asks.

We all shrug.

'Daniel Hastie is marrying a professional rock climber,' Bella says. 'Don't you see? For my spew-worthy class project, I could design a wedding outfit for a *rock climber*. And they want somewhere weird. They could do it on top of Hangman's Peak! She'll need special shoes, pants, maybe some abseiling gear…'

We all start talking at once and don't notice at first that Dr Singh is clicking her fingers and trying to get our attention.

'Bella,' she says. 'Girls, I might be able to help you with this.'

We pause and listen to Dr Singh.

'I know the manager of the Harbour View Hotel,' she says. 'I performed an operation on his spinal cord. He wouldn't be able to walk if it wasn't for that procedure. I could see if he'd be willing to arrange a meeting between us and the bride-to-be. We could pitch the idea of a mountain-top wedding and offer up your design skills, Bella!'

The anti-princesses squeal in utter joy.

'I can't wait until we get back to the treehouse, I want to propose a mission right now,' Bella says. 'Is that okay, Ms President?'

Emily nods with a smile.

'Mission Bride: Design a wedding outfit for Svetlana…what was her name?' Bella asks.

I yell excitedly: 'KARPINSKAIA!'

Bella yells back: 'All in favour?!'

Chloe, Emily and I raise our hands so quickly they hit the roof of the car.

'I'll start sketching right away,' Bella says. 'I'll have some drawings ready for Svetlana to choose from. She won't be able to resist.'

We hum the Wedding March all the way home to Bella's.

CHaPTeR SIXTEEN

I sprint across the front lawn like a gazelle.

'Mum, Dad!' I yell. 'Tom, Harry!'

They're all in the kitchen packing food into containers.

'Hi, Grace,' Mum says. 'We're going to the hospital to have dinner with Oliver.'

I thought the anti-princesses looked mopey this afternoon, but my family is worse.

'I have some exciting news to tell you first,' I say. 'It's about Manchester United.'

Dad slams his fist on the sink. The noise shocks Mum and she drops a tub of salad on the floor.

'We need to forget about Manchester United, Grace,' Dad says. 'It will drive us all insane to keep thinking about it.'

Tom's throat wobbles. He's not ready to give up, and neither am I.

'But Dad, I found out where they're staying,' I say. 'They're at the Harbour View Hotel in town.'

Harry claps his hands in delight. 'We could stalk them! When they come out we could tell them what happened to Oliver. I bet they'd give us tickets if they knew our story.'

Dad helps Mum pick up lettuce leaves. 'Look, kids, I'm sorry to let you down,' he says. 'But don't you realise there'd be at least another dozen people who missed out on tickets with sob stories just like ours?'

Surely Mum will see the light.

'Mum, come on,' I say. 'It's our last chance.'

She bites her lip.

Harry and Tom look at her anxiously.

'Your dad is right,' she says. 'We need to

move on, if not for ourselves then for Oliver's sake. He blames himself for our missing out on the tickets. When we get to the hospital I don't want to hear another word about it. He's in enough pain as it is.'

I slump onto a stool and lay my head on the kitchen bench.

'This is SO unfair!' Tom yells, and storms off to his room with Harry.

I grab a pen and a piece of paper from next to the telephone and start to scribble madly.

Dear Manchester United players,
My name is Grace Bennett and I want you to know that my family and I are your biggest fans.
Unfortunately, we missed out on tickets to the big game in Newcastle as my brother Oliver broke his ankle...

Mum and Dad might not want us to talk about the game anymore, but they didn't say anything about writing.

I vow to get that letter to the Harbour View Hotel. It just may be the ticket to completing Mission ManU.

INGREDIENTS:
2 cups distilled water
3 tablespoons alcohol
5 drops lavender oil
10 drops rosemary oil
3 rosemary sprigs

'Oh no,' Chloe says. 'Apparently, this is a perfume recipe.'

I take the piece of paper from her hand.

'Mr Ashton handed these out just before the recess bell,' Chloe says. 'I guess it's further instruction for my assignment.'

Mr Ashton spots us on our way to the picnic table and calls out, 'What do you think, Chloe? It's basic, but a popular combination.'

Matt Vernon, who's in Chloe and Bella's class, is walking two steps behind us. 'Mr Ashton, would it be okay if we didn't do the exact experiment we've been allocated?' he asks. 'I'm not sure this rocket is what I want to make.'

Chloe doesn't need to hear that twice. She turns around to swap her perfume recipe with Matt's instructions.

'Of course you don't need to follow those instructions rigidly,' Mr Ashton says. 'In fact, I'll be awarding extra marks to those who think outside the box.'

Matt and Chloe frown, confused. What was the point of the whole boy-girl thing if they could choose their own experiment?

'So, can I make perfume?' Matt asks. 'Because I've got a great idea for a vanilla and bergamot blend.'

Mr Ashton holds his belly and laughs. 'Good one,' he says. 'No, what I mean is, if you can make a bigger, better rocket than the one I've given you instructions for, you could top the class. Same goes for the girls. If you can make an original perfume from your own recipe, you'll earn a better mark.'

Mr Ashton still thinks science comes in pink and blue.

'I also have an exciting announcement I'll be making in class,' he continues. 'How would you like to be the first to know?'

Chloe and Matt clearly couldn't care less. Mr Ashton's announcements have so far been major let-downs.

'Oh, all right, I'll tell you,' he says. 'We'll be unveiling these projects at a special open day that your families will be invited to. Won't that be grand?'

I cover my mouth and try not to laugh. The thought of Chloe presenting a bottle of sweet-smelling perfume to her parents and Yiayia is pretty funny. They would be as confused as we are to see Chloe fiddling with a delicate bottle of rosemary and lavender.

'Just great, Mr Ashton,' Chloe says. 'See you in class.'

I giggle as Chloe's teacher waddles away.

'He doesn't know what he's in for,' Chloe says. 'I'll be kicking up quite a stink at that open day. Quite a stink.'

If her practice run involved eggs and vinegar, I don't doubt my friend's words.

CHAPTER EIGHTEEN

It's time to say goodbye to Emily's baby.

Bella, Chloe and I gather around Emily as she sits in front of the computer. This must be the hardest thing she's ever done.

'I'd better explain myself to the anti-princesses first, I suppose,' she says. 'So I don't get bombarded in the playground.'

Emily opens the Anti-Princess Club website and logs into her chatroom.

ANTI-PRINCESS CLUB MATHS CHAT

MEMBERS ONLINE: 217   MODERATOR: Emily Martin

Emily is online

ANNABELLE: Did you hear about Rachel Cirlin? I heard she's grounded for coming to school with red spray paint in her hair.

ELISE: Oh, that's not what I heard. Felix told me she got caught stealing five dollars from her mother's purse.

ALLEGRA: She wouldn't do that, she's my friend.

VIOLET: Annabelle, you're so nasty for even bringing it up.

ANNABELLE: Hey, I'm just saying what I heard.

Emily throws her hands in the air and turns to the rest of us. 'What has this become? The gossip almost makes me *want* to shut it down. I don't want to moderate something like this.'

EMILY: Hello, everyone. I'm afraid I have some bad news.

ELISE: ??

EMILY: I'm really ashamed of what's become of this chatroom. It was supposed to be a place where anti-princesses logged on for help with their maths homework.

AISHA: Emily, Emily, I'm here! I need help with a geometry question.

EMILY: It's too late for that, Aisha. This chatroom has been abused. It's turned into a place of useless gossip. And I must say I'm surprised at how mean a lot of you are on here. I can't imagine you speaking this way to each other in person.

ALLEGRA: We're sorry, Emily. We'll go back to chatting about maths.

EMILY: Like I said, Allegra, it's too late. I've been ordered to pull the site down.

VIOLET: No!

AISHA: Don't do it, Emily!

ELISE: I'm new here, I didn't do anything! Please leave it up!

EMILY: It's coming down. Principal's orders. Goodbye, girls.

🔘 Emily is offline.

Emily blows her nose and slumps. Bella rubs her back while I pass her a glass of water.

'You've got to do it,' I say. 'We don't want you in any more trouble with Mrs O'Neill.'

Emily brings up a page of coding the rest of us don't understand. She starts typing and her sniffles become more intense.

'Wait,' Chloe says. 'What if you didn't *completely* take it down? You could just temporarily disable it, couldn't you?'

Emily nods. 'Well, yes,' she says. 'But why would I do that?'

Chloe lifts up three fingers. 'We've come up with a mission to help Bella, another for Grace and a third for me. I think it's time we set a mission for you, Emily.'

Emily runs her fingers across the keyboard. 'I can't propose a mission to keep the website up,' she says. 'I'd be in detention every lunchtime for the rest of the year.'

Bella clicks her fingers. She's had a lightbulb moment. 'Reconstruct!' she yells. 'Rebuild the website. Write an anti-gossip code or something. You know what you're doing.'

Emily wipes her eyes and straightens her shoulders. She grins as she starts typing again.

A white screen pops up with a red message scrolling through the centre.

SITE UNDERGOING MAINTENANCE.

'That should do it,' Emily says. 'The nuts and bolts are still there, as you would say, Bella. But no one can get in. For now, anyway.' She swings around to face us. 'I guess I don't need to ask if you're all in favour, then?'

We throw our arms around Emily in a massive group hug.

We're not saying farewell to the baby after all. It's being reborn.

Mission Rebirth: Create new and improved Anti-Princess Club website.

CHAPTER NINETEEN

The Harbour View Hotel is one of the tallest buildings in Newcastle. As Dr Singh pulls up across the road, I wonder which floors the ManU players are on. Probably the top.

'Ready, girls?' Dr Singh asks. 'The manager's name is Mr James, okay?'

Bella hugs her sketchpad to her chest and grins like a Cheshire cat.

'Now, he's organised a five-minute meeting for us with Svetlana Karpinskaia, but no more than that,' Dr Singh says. 'So, we need to be succinct and not get too excited, okay?'

I'm clutching my letter to Manchester

United, hoping my palms aren't sweating too heavily on the paper. 'Um, Dr Singh? I have a letter for Manchester United. Do you think Mr James could organise a meeting with them too?'

'That may be pushing our luck, Grace,' Dr Singh says. 'I think we'll have to settle for Svetlana Karpinskaia.'

I'm determined to get that letter into the hands of ManU somehow. 'What are the chances of the players being here now, Emily?' I ask. 'You know, from a mathematical perspective.'

Emily screws up her face. 'I'm afraid I can't work that out accurately,' she says. 'There are too many unknown variables. Are they even staying in Newcastle tonight? Maybe they're training out of town. Are they together or separated?'

'Okay, let's go in,' I say. 'I guess I can leave the letter at reception and hope it'll be passed on.'

Emily gives me a wink. 'What I *can* predict is that there's a far greater chance of the hotel staff passing the letter on to one of the players than you coming into contact with one of them yourself.'

Dr Singh greets the doorman and he lets us in without hesitation. A huge chandelier hangs from the foyer ceiling and a marble staircase curls up to the second floor. 'Wowee,' Bella says. 'This place is a work of art.'

Dr Singh leads us to the concierge. 'We have a meeting with the manager, Mr James—'

'Dr Singh!' a voice calls out from a doorway near the base of the stairwell.

Bella's mum waves to a bearded man in a fancy suit. At his side is a tall, blonde woman in jeans and a T-shirt.

We follow Dr Singh over to the pair.

'Girls, this is Mr James,' Dr Singh says.

'Welcome,' he says. 'May I introduce you all to Ms Karpinskaia.'

The blonde woman extends her hand to each of us. 'Lovely to meet you,' she says in a Russian accent. 'Are you girls rock-climbing fans?'

Bella tells a white lie. 'Yes, I love rock-climbing,' she says. 'In fact, it gave me the idea that you should get married at a mountain called Hangman's Peak. We heard on the radio that you hadn't chosen a wedding spot.'

Svetlana laughs. 'I've actually just returned from Hangman's Peak,' she says. 'It was a great climb, but I don't really want to get married on a mountain. I'm always climbing mountains.'

Bella thinks fast. 'What about a lovely church?' she asks. 'There are loads of examples of great architecture around Newcastle.'

Svetlana yawns and inspects her fingernails. 'I'm not religious,' she says. 'Daniel and I want something a little more…exciting. So, do you have any questions about rock-climbing?'

I pinch Bella on the leg.

'What about a bridge?' Bella asks. 'The harbour bridge. It's at least a hundred metres high. I bet no one has ever got married on top.'

Svetlana stares at Bella curiously. She cocks her head to one side and begins to whisper, 'Yes, yes, yes.' Her whisper turns to a little squeal. She claps her hands and jumps up and down – just like we do when we're excited. 'The harbour bridge sounds *perfect*! And it would be such a beautiful spot at sunset.'

Svetlana turns to Mr James. 'Could you help me find a celebrant willing to climb the bridge?' she asks. 'I hope we haven't left it too late…March fifth is so close.'

Mr James starts punching a number into his mobile phone. 'I'm sure there are plenty of celebrants who would be more than willing to climb a bridge to marry such a famous couple.'

Svetlana claps again.

I reach into my pocket. 'I have this letter for Manchester United,' I say. 'Do you think you could pass it on?'

Svetlana frowns. I think she's sensed that I'm more interested in soccer than rock-climbing. 'Sure,' she says unconvincingly as I pass her the letter.

'Okay, well, it was lovely to have you here, girls,' Mr James says. 'But Ms Karpinskaia is on a tight schedule.'

Bella opens her sketchbook. 'Wait, I have one more thing to show you.'

Mr James ushers Svetlana to the staircase.

'I've designed you a wedding outfit,' Bella says. 'It's right here!'

Svetlana calls back to Bella, 'Sorry, sweetheart, but Donatella Almasi insists I wear one of her designs – she's friends with Daniel.'

As we walk back to the grand doorway, Dr Singh rests her hand on Bella's shoulder. 'Donatella Almasi is a famous fashion designer. But you could still make your design for your class project, Bella. It doesn't matter if Svetlana doesn't wear it.'

'I'm not giving up,' Bella whispers. 'I think she's a size ten. Do you think she wants to wear white?'

I take a last look back at Svetlana.

Then it happens.

She hands my letter to Mr James and disappears at the top of the staircase.

CHAPTER

Yes, we got into the Harbour View Hotel. Yes, we met Svetlana Karpinskaia. Yes, we found out when and where she's going to marry Manchester United striker Daniel Hastie.

I go over the list of yeses in my head as I sprint around the school oval. I've left Bella and Chloe on their own for lunch while Emily's in detention. I need some time to think and I do that best when I'm running.

I figure I can't rely on Mr James passing my letter on to the team. I need to come up with another way to get those tickets.

'It's not the end,' I tell myself. 'There's still

six days to the game.'

The bell rings and I jog back to class.

Everyone's standing outside. The classroom door is locked and there's a blue and red sign on it.

'What could it mean?' Emily asks. 'New Jersey? Nice job? No joke? Norma Jean?'

There's only one NJ that comes to my mind. 'Emily, I've got it!' I say. 'We were wrong to be targeting Manchester United for tickets. We should've gone to our home team – the Newcastle Jets!'

Mr Talbot claws through the crowd. He's wearing a red and blue Jets jersey.

'Good afternoon, all,' he says. 'Ready to come inside and find out what's going on?'

Everyone screams: 'Yes!'

Mr Talbot opens the door and we spill into the classroom. It's covered in streamers and posters. There are even soccer balls rolling around on the floor.

'Take your seats, everyone,' he says. 'I've got an announcement to make.'

My butt hits my chair so quickly it sends a jolt up my spine. Emily takes her seat beside me and I squeeze her hand.

'Ouch, Grace!' she says. 'You're stronger than you realise.'

Mr Talbot does a mock drumroll on his desk with his palms. 'The best soccer team in the world, the Newcastle Jets, has come to me with an amazing opportunity.'

I start sweating. I'm breathing hard and fast. I may hyperventilate.

'They're looking for six students to perform during half-time at Newcastle Stadium when they play Manchester United,' he says. 'So, I'm organising tryouts for anyone who wants to during lunchtime this Friday.'

Emily slaps me on the back. 'You're in, Grace! You're the best player in the whole school!'

I can't believe my luck. Could it really be so easy?

I throw my hand up.

'Yes, Grace?' Mr Talbot asks.

I stutter as I try to get my words out. 'I'm just…I'm…so excited…so…just wondering…'

Mr Talbot waits patiently until I get myself together.

'If we are chosen,' I blurt, 'can we bring our families along?'

I cross my fingers as Mr Talbot scans his notes. 'Yes,' he says at last. 'You'll receive a family pass.'

I knock over our desk as I jump into the air. I bounce so high, the ceiling fan skims the top of my hair.

I missed out on my first two chances for tickets, and now I've got a third. This won't be a case of three strikes and out. It's all up to me.

CHAPTER TWENTY-ONE

This should be a blast – literally.

Bella, Emily and I are sitting with Yiayia in the school playground.

We're waiting for Chloe to present her science project to an audience of at least fifty parents, teachers and other fifth-graders.

'I hope my granddaughter does not get into trouble for this,' Yiayia says.

I giggle and point to Mr Ashton. 'I guess it depends on him.'

Mr Ashton introduces himself to the crowd. 'Welcome to this special event,' he says. 'To begin the school year we're showing off the unique skills and passions of our students.'

Bella and Emily groan. Mr Ashton is absolutely clueless.

'First up we have the very great pleasure of meeting some of our top scientists, then we'll move on to other areas such as geography, mathematics and even fashion design,' he says. 'Let's give them a round of applause.'

The audience claps and I lean into Bella. 'What are you going to do when it's your turn?'

'Show the class what I've designed for Svetlana,' she says. 'And I'm taking it along on Saturday, even though Donatella What's-her-name has already designed an outfit.'

Chloe, two other girls and four boys line up in front of us.

The other girls are holding small bottles, the boys have rockets, and Chloe is standing by a large crate with a sheet draped over it.

'I've had a peek at some of these projects,' Mr Ashton says. 'But not all of them. So even I'm in for a treat today. Let's start with you, Matt.'

Matt steps forward with his rocket. 'Well, it's made from a drinking straw, paper and sticky tape,' he says. 'I rolled the paper around the straw, folded the top down and stuck it with tape. Then I pulled the straw out.'

Mr Ashton nods along but he is only semi-impressed by the paper cylinder. 'And does it fly?'

Matt seems to have forgotten that part. 'Oh, yeah. Like this.'

He slides the paper rocket onto the straw and uses his mouth to blow through the end. It pops off and into the air.

Matt's mother cheers supportively while the rest of the audience half-heartedly claps.

'Poor Matt,' Bella whispers. 'He wanted to make perfume for his mum.'

A hush sweeps over the crowd as Mrs O'Neill arrives at the presentation and takes a seat next to Yiayia.

'Oh good, the principal is here,' Mr Ashton says. 'I think you'll enjoy the next project, Mrs O'Neill. Daisy Northcott is our next student.'

Daisy holds up her bottle and smiles awkwardly. 'This is my perfume. It's made from rosemary, lavender, water and alcohol.'

Mr Ashton nudges her towards the audience. 'Hand the bottle around for our guests to smell, Daisy,' he says.

Daisy passes her concoction to Yiayia, and I catch Mrs O'Neill yawning.

'Chloe Karalis, you're next,' Mr Ashton says.

Bella, Emily and I hoot as Chloe pulls the sheet off her crate.

She has built a rocket that's as tall as her shoulders. It's metallic, with four tailfins, a cone-shaped nose and a huge NASA sticker on the side.

Mr Ashton shakes his head with such force, he sends his droopy cheeks flapping like a bloodhound's. 'Chloe, you were supposed to make perfume, remember?'

The crowd begins to murmur. I can already hear a few hints of disapproval over the girl– boy divide.

'It's okay, Mr Ashton,' Chloe says. 'I have made a fragrance. This rocket is just what you'd call the dispenser, I suppose.'

Mr Ashton narrows his eyes and steps back cautiously.

'Let me start by telling you about the rocket,' Chloe says. 'It's made from a plastic canister, cardboard and tape.' She pulls a glass bottle and a bag of white powder from the crate. 'And this is the perfume. Also known as rocket fuel.'

A few of the parents at the back of the crowd stand to watch Chloe as she tips the powder into the canister part of the rocket.

'Now, I'm going to have to ask you all to keep clear,' she says. 'This baby is about to take off.'

Everyone takes a few steps back as Chloe pours the liquid from her bottle into the canister. She seals it quickly and jumps away from the rocket.

It takes about four seconds for the rocket

to launch. It flies so high it clears the tops of the closest trees and we lose sight of it until it hits the ground.

'Woooooohoooooo!' Bella, Emily and I yell. 'Go Chloe!'

Mr Ashton stands up and signals for everyone to be quiet. 'While that was a very good example of a bicarb soda and vinegar rocket, Chloe, I'm afraid you failed to make the perfume as instructed.'

Some dads up the back boo.

Then it comes.

Yiayia pulls out a handkerchief and covers her nose with it.

'*What is that stench?*' one of the mums calls out.

I pinch my nostrils. Bella pulls her shirt up over her nose. Emily starts to cough. We're surrounded by people gagging, spluttering and covering their faces.

'You're right, Mr Ashton,' Chloe says. 'It *is* a bicarb soda and vinegar-powered rocket. But I added an ingredient to fulfil the perfume assignment.'

Mr Ashton's cheeks have blown up like balloons.

'Rotten eggs,' Chloe declares. 'Mixed with vinegar, they make a very strong perfume, don't you think?'

Mr Ashton grabs his stomach and runs

away towards the classroom. He covers his mouth with his hand as he goes.

'He's going to spew,' I say to Bella.

The parents begin to whisper, while a few of the kids giggle, and Mrs O'Neill stands up to address the crowd.

'I'm afraid we may have to take a raincheck on those other presentations until Mr Ashton is feeling a little better,' she says. 'Thank you for coming, and we'll let you know when we can resume.'

Mission Blast-Off: complete.

CHAPTER TWENTY-TWO

Mrs O'Neill's familiar drawl reverberates through the school's sound system.

'Attention, students. Please make your way to the library at the end of your lunch break. Normal classes will be postponed for twenty minutes as teachers attend an emergency meeting.'

A bunch of fourth-graders high-five each other near our picnic table. The school librarian is a pushover, so they're excited at the possibility of misbehaving for twenty minutes.

'I wonder what the emergency is,' Bella says. 'Something terribly important like running out of whiteboard markers, I suppose.'

Chloe and I giggle at Bella's joke. The sad thing is, we've lost a bit of faith in our teachers. Bumbling Mr Ashton is still reeling after Chloe's rancid rocket stunt, and Mrs O'Neill is making Emily pay for the nastiness on her website with a string of detentions.

'Hey, let's go meet Emily after her detention,' I say. 'We can walk to the library together.'

We all grab our backpacks and stroll to the room where our president is serving her time.

I peek through the window.

Mrs O'Neill is talking to Emily.

Bella, Chloe and I press our ears up to the gap between the glass and the bricks.

'We have a problem, Emily,' Mrs O'Neill says. 'My staff are feeling a little…well… overwhelmed.'

Emily listens quietly.

'They're experiencing what I'd describe as an influx of extra maths-related queries since the disabling of your website,' Mrs O'Neill says. 'It's contributing significantly to their workloads.'

It doesn't take Emily long to put two and two together. 'I did do a lot of tutoring on the Anti-Princess Club website,' she says. 'It actually got a little out of control.'

Mrs O'Neill leans against the edge of Emily's desk and takes off her glasses. 'Do you want to rebuild the website, Emily?'

That's a no-brainer. 'Yes, I do,' Emily says. 'But a new, improved version.'

Mrs O'Neill paces across the room, scratching her chin just like Emily does when she's thinking. 'I've got an idea,' she says. 'You can rebuild the site with the school's support.'

Emily narrows her eyes. 'What does "the school's support" mean?'

'Let's put it in writing.' Mrs O'Neill opens her briefcase and removes a laptop. She fires it up, plugs in a printer and starts typing.

Emily spots us at the window and beams.

Mrs O'Neill finishes typing and the printer beeps and whirs. She takes the freshly printed document and slides it across the desk to Emily.

'Read it out loud!' Bella calls.

Chloe and I look at Bella in shock. 'What are you thinking?' I hiss.

Mrs O'Neill walks over to the window. 'Well, well,' she says, opening it fully. 'We have some spies on our hands. Come on in, then, anti-princesses.'

Chloe, Bella and I run into the detention room. We all gather around Emily as she reads Mrs O'Neill's proposition.

Emily Martin,

Newcastle Public School would like to offer you paid employment as an online tutor in the field of mathematics.

Remuneration for the above-mentioned position is to be $15 per hour.

Newcastle Public School teachers with maths expertise will help with the tutoring.

Further conditions are open for discussion.

Sincerely,
Gretchen O'Neill,
Principal, Newcastle Public School

'Congratulations.' I pat Emily on the back. 'You get to resurrect the website *and* get paid for it.'

Emily crosses her arms and looks Mrs O'Neill in the eye. It's negotiation time.

'No more detention,' Emily says.

'No more detention,' Mrs O'Neill says.

'I remain the chatroom's head moderator.'

'You're the boss.'

'I'm going to write up a code of conduct that stamps out gossiping.'

'Sounds fantastic.'

Emily types in the Anti-Princess Club web address along with some code. The 'site undergoing maintenance' message appears and Emily replaces it with a new line.

New and improved Anti-Princess Club website – COMING SOON.

Mission Rebirth: complete.

CHAPTER TWENTY-THREE

Don't be too cocky. Don't be too cocky.

I repeat my mantra quietly.

I know I'm one of the best athletes at school, but everyone here is super determined. Attitude could be the deciding factor that snags me one of the six spots to play at half-time during the Manchester United match.

'Good luck, Grace,' Bella says. 'We'll be watching from the grandstand.'

I hug the anti-princesses and focus on my competition. There are more than a hundred kids warming up around me. My brothers – except for Oliver – are among them.

Mr Talbot addresses the crowd with a megaphone. 'You've got half an hour to show us your skills,' he says. 'Five stations are set up around the field. It's up to you how long you spend at each and in which order you approach them, but we'll be looking for well-rounded performers with skills in as many areas as possible.'

Five stations in half an hour. That's six minutes per station. I set my watch.

'At one station you'll dribble the ball through a set of cones using only your left foot,' Mr Talbot says. 'At another you will need to head a ball as many times as you can before it touches the ground. At the southern net you will be goal-shooting. At the northern nets you'll be goalkeeping. And at the station closest to the grandstand I want to see your dance moves.'

The crowd erupts in laughter. 'I'm serious, people,' Mr Talbot says. 'At the fifth station, there will be music playing and you'll be required to dance. If you choose to, that is.'

Tom and Harry are horrified. I can't say I'm entirely impressed either, but after Mum and Dad forcing me to do ballet for years I find my brothers' reaction kind of amusing.

Tom waves at Mr Talbot. 'Um, sir,' he says. 'Why the dancing?'

Mr Talbot is deliberately mysterious. 'Why not?' He raises his whistle to his lips and yells: 'On your marks, get set, GO!'

We scatter across the field like desperate cockroaches.

I start the timer on my watch and head straight for the cones. 'Just the left foot,' I whisper to myself. 'Keep the right foot back.'

My watch beeps and I leave about a dozen kids behind at the cones as I run to the heading station. I chip a ball into the air and start bouncing it off my forehead. My eyes are fixed on the ball as it bounces up and down.

Five, six, seven, eight...forty-nine, fifty.

My forehead goes numb, but there's no way that ball is hitting the ground.

The beep of my watch brings me out of my trance. I let the ball fall into my arms and run to the next station.

I line up to take my turn shooting at the goal. Tom is a couple of kickers ahead of me and misses completely. 'Darn it!' he yells and trudges to the back of the line.

I get to the ball and pull back my right foot. There's no need to shoot high, so I lean forward to keep the ball low to the ground. The instep of my boot strikes the leather and the ball curves slightly. It glides across the grass and into the goal.

'Go, Grace!' Emily yells. 'Nice shot!'

I wave to the grandstand as my watch beeps.

I decide to save the worst for last and sprint to the other end of the field. There's a motorised ball launcher set up in front of the goal. It must be shooting at top speed, because no one is managing to stop the balls.

'My turn!' I yell. I take my place in front of the posts and wait for the machine to spit.

A ball flies above my head and I leap into the air. I arch my back and stretch my fingers. I catch it and roll it away as the next ball shoots across the ground. I slide through some mud and stop the ball with the tips of my toes. Just.

Beep, beep, beep. Beep. Beep.

I run to the last station, but there's no one else there. Either they got their dancing done early or they're too focused on the soccer drills.

A cheesy disco song starts up and I step from side to side. I see Chloe in the grandstand running her finger across her throat – it's the 'cut it' signal.

Impressive dance moves aren't my forte.

I spy a ball out of the corner of my eye. Maybe I could use it as a prop.

I pick it up, lift it above my head and drop into the splits. Then I swing my legs around and throw the ball into the air as I do a backward roll. As I land, I put the ball between my feet and do a handstand.

There are cheers from the grandstand, but

I worry that what I'm doing is more of a rhythmic gymnastics routine than dancing.

My watch beeps for the final time and I do a pirouette. Finally, those dreaded ballet lessons have actually come in handy for something.

'Time's up!' Mr Talbot calls. 'I'll be reviewing your performances this evening and contacting the successful students tomorrow.'

A few faces drop as everyone realises we won't find out the results immediately.

'The bell will ring any second now, so let's all head back to class,' Mr Talbot says. 'Except you, Grace – a moment, please?'

I stay put as Emily, Bella and Chloe leave the grandstand. Maybe Mr Talbot wants me to help him pack up the equipment.

'Grace Bennett,' he says. 'You're in.'

Mr Talbot's words don't register.

'Excuse me?' I ask.

He starts to collect the cones. 'You're in, Grace,' he says. 'No need to wait until tomorrow. You're the only one who danced. Automatic qualification. Although, I must say you were one of the best all round.'

I'm frozen in disbelief.

'Better get to class,' Mr Talbot says. 'Your teacher knows where you are.'

I skip down the grandstand steps and collapse in a heap at the bottom.

'You okay, Grace?' Mr Talbot asks.

I start crying. I've heard people do this when they're overwhelmed with happiness.

'Thank you, Mr Talbot,' I blubber. 'Thank you.'

Mission ManU: complete.

CHAPTER TWENTY-FOUR

The paparazzi's cameras are flashing while TV reporters interview fans of Daniel Hastie.

A woman with big, stiff hair sticks a microphone under my nose. 'Care to tell us why you're here today?'

The pressure to speak on the spot to a stranger makes me uncomfortable. 'I, ah, I,' I stutter. 'I'm a big, big soccer nut.'

The reporter moves on to a nearby family in Manchester United jerseys.

Bella is beginning to stress out. 'We need to get closer to the base of the bridge,' she says. 'But the crowd is too thick.'

Bella's mum has a brainwave. 'Miss Journalist!' she yells. 'We have a story for you!'

The reporter looks sceptical and keeps interviewing the other family.

'It's about Svetlana's dress!' Bella shouts.

Three news crews swarm around us. 'What can you tell us about the dress?' asks one reporter. 'Can you confirm the designer as Donatella Almasi?' asks another.

I point to the coathanger and zip-up bag draped over Bella's shoulder. 'It's in there. Bella is the designer. She's only ten, you know.'

Two crews walk away immediately.

The stiff-haired reporter shakes her head. 'You had me there for a minute.'

Bella grabs the reporter's wrist as she turns away. 'It *is* a wedding outfit,' she says. 'I designed it for Svetlana so she'd be able to climb the bridge. I've brought it along just in case she's not happy with her dress – I researched Donatella Almasi's style and it's not exactly practical.'

'That could be a nice little scoop,' the

cameraman says quietly to the reporter. 'It won't matter if she doesn't take the kid's dress.'

The reporter looks Bella up and down and makes a 'hmmmmmm' sound. 'All right,' she says. 'Come with us, kids. We'll take you to the media scrum.'

I link arms with Bella, Emily, Chloe and Dr Singh. We weave through the crowd behind the TV crew until we reach a red rope and a row of security guards.

The reporter holds up a plastic card on a lanyard. 'They're with me.'

A guard unhooks a piece of rope and ushers us through.

'Just in time,' Dr Singh says. 'Here they are.'

A white limousine slowly pulls up a few metres away from us. Daniel gets out first and waves to the crowd. Svetlana is next.

'Just as I thought,' Bella says. 'A completely impractical design.'

Daniel is wearing a climbing harness over his suit, while Svetlana has one pulled over a ballgown that makes her look like one of those birthday cakes with a doll in the middle.

The reporters are screaming at the couple, but they ignore the fuss and head to the bridge steps.

Daniel starts the climb first and extends his hand to help Svetlana. She squeezes onto the narrow staircase, squashing her dress to half the width so she can fit.

Our reporter turns to Bella with the camera rolling. 'As you can see, viewers, Svetlana is wearing a signature Almasi ballgown for her bridge-top ceremony. But we're here with a budding young designer who had been hoping to present the rock climber with a more functional ensemble.'

Bella confidently takes the microphone. 'My name is Bella Singh,' she says. 'I'm here today because I've designed a wedding outfit especially for bridge-climbing. I wanted Svetlana Karpinskaia to wear it.'

The reporter looks impressed. 'Why don't you show the viewers what you've got there?'

Bella unzips the bag, fumbling a little as a gust of wind blows her hair across her face.

'*Help!*' a piercing scream comes from the bridge.

Svetlana is halfway up the steps, her dress billowing around her like a parachute.

'It's the wind,' Bella says. 'It's caught under her skirt.'

'She's coming down!' about twenty reporters call at once.

We push Bella to the very front of the press pack. She pulls a white jumpsuit and cape from her bag.

About half of the paparazzi now have their cameras pointing at us.

'Over here, Svetlana!' I call. 'It's us! From the hotel!'

Bella is waving Svetlana's jumpsuit through the air like a big white flag.

Svetlana reaches the bottom of the steps and gazes in our direction for a split second. She heads towards the limo, then stops and

looks back, cocking her head to the side in the same way she did when Bella suggested the bridge-top ceremony.

'Here she comes!' Chloe yells. 'She's coming over to us!'

Svetlana and Daniel walk hand-in-hand to the edge of the media pit. A few reporters shove microphones under their noses, but Daniel pushes them away.

'These are the girls I was telling you about, Daniel!' Svetlana says. 'They suggested the bridge.' She turns to us. 'I can't make it up the stairs in this thing I'm wearing.'

Bella practically throws the jumpsuit at the bride. 'This is the outfit,' she says. 'It's a jumpsuit and it's weatherproof and has plenty of stretch – perfect for climbing.'

Svetlana takes the cape. 'And what is this? A veil?'

'No,' Bella scoffs. 'It's a cape, you know, like superheroes wear. But I guess you could put it on your head if you wanted to be weird.'

For the first time since we arrived, the crowd has gone quiet. Everyone is waiting to see whether Svetlana will wear Bella's gear.

'I tell you what,' Svetlana says. 'Daniel will put the names of you and your friends at the gate for tomorrow's game in exchange for this design of yours.'

Bella shrieks with joy. 'My friend Grace already has tickets,' she says. 'But the rest of us would love to go.'

Svetlana kisses Bella on both cheeks. 'You've saved the day,' she says. 'If you're ever in a bind, I hope a clever person just like you can come to your rescue.'

I giggle as I guess what Bella's about to say next.

'Thanks, but I don't need rescuing,' Bella says.

Svetlana cocks her head to one side again and takes one last curious look at Bella before taking her outfit into the limo to get changed.

Our reporter raises Bella's arm as though she's a boxer who's just won a bout. 'She's done it! Daniel Hastie and Svetlana Karpinskaia will live happily ever after thanks to ten-year-old Bella Singh.'

Bella throws a peace sign for the cameras, then takes her mum's hand. 'Let's go.'

Dr Singh points at the bridge. 'Don't you want to see the wedding?'

Bella looks to the rest of us and we screw up our noses.

'No thanks, Mum,' Bella says. 'We're done here. Weddings are a bit spew-worthy.'

Mission Bride: complete.

CHAPTER TWENTY-FIVE

There are tickets for Very Important People.
Then there are Very Very Important People's
tickets.

My family and the other anti-princesses are
in the VIP section of the stadium. I caught a
glimpse of them cheering madly in the first
half of the game, but I wasn't allowed to sit
with them. The kids performing at half-time
are VVIPs.

There are about thirty of us who have been
specially selected from around Newcastle. I'm
the only girl from Newcastle Public but there
are five from other schools – the other twenty-

four kids are boys. You can't tell who's from where though, because we've all been given Jets jerseys to wear.

'I can't believe I'm going to be playing soccer at Newcastle Stadium,' I say to a boy sitting nearby. 'I wonder if the professional players will be watching.'

The boy is about to say something when a man wearing a headset appears in our booth. 'Okay, kids, time to head down to the green room,' he says. 'We've got fifteen minutes before the show.'

I take a deep breath and savour every step through the halls. Next time I'm here I'll probably be one of the grown-up athletes.

We get to the green room and see five adults in Jets uniforms – four men and one woman. They're each holding a placard numbered from one to five.

The man in the headset stands on a box. 'Attention, please,' he says. 'You're all wearing wristbands. Please check the number on your band, then line up behind the person holding the same number.'

I check my wrist. Five. That's the woman's number. I take my place behind her. The other girls in the group do the same. The boys line up in groups of six behind the men.

I have a weird feeling about this.

'Good job,' the man in the headset says. 'Now, you all participated in a series of drills to qualify for today's show. You'll each be performing one of those drills on the field.'

This isn't good. It's not good at all.

'Excuse me,' I interrupt the man. 'I thought we were playing an actual soccer game.'

He makes a muffled 'grrrrrr' sound into his headset's microphone. 'I'm afraid there must have been a communication problem at your end,' he says. 'You only have ten minutes on the field before the second half of the real game resumes. You couldn't get a match played in that time.'

I try to interrupt again, but he holds his

hand up to my face. 'No more questions. We're on a tight schedule here.'

The man hands bags of soccer balls to the leader of every group – except mine. Instead of balls, he passes what looks like a giant bag of feathers to the woman.

'What is that?' I whisper to a girl next to me.

She stares at me as though I'm an imbecile. 'Duh. They're pompoms.'

My skin starts to heat up. So this is what it feels like when your blood boils.

The man claps his hands. 'No time for chatter,' he says. 'Now – Group One, you'll be dribbling the ball through some cones. Group Two is heading balls. Three will be goal-shooting. Four, goalkeeping. Five, cheerleading.'

I think I'm going to pass out. I'm not here to jiggle pompoms. I thought that dance station at tryouts was a curve-ball to test our pluck.

I follow the others down the tunnel to the field, lost in a daze. Should I pull out completely?

Then I hear it: the sound of cleats on cement.

I lift my head and see them. The real-life Manchester United and Newcastle Jets players running towards us on their way to the dressing-rooms.

My left arm shoots out automatically and the players start to high-five me. I'm in awe as each sweaty palm slaps mine.

'Good game,' I say over and over. Some smile, some nod, some don't make eye contact at all.

Daniel Hastie is the last to come off.

'Good game,' I say again. 'And congrats on the wedding.'

He stops and shakes my hand. 'Thanks, buddy. Show us what you got out there, huh?'

That's it. I will. I'll use every one of those ten minutes to show them what I've got.

I'm blinded a little by the lights as we run onto the field. I wave aimlessly, hoping my family and the anti-princesses can make me out.

Our group leader takes us onto the centre

spot and passes us two pompoms each.

As I grab mine, I reach down and set my watch's timer for two minutes.

'Copy me!' our leader says. She starts kicking her legs in the air as though she's a can-can dancer.

If I'm going to do this, I may as well make it memorable. I ignore the instructions and do a cartwheel followed by the splits. I jump up and throw in a pirouette to give my mum and dad a laugh.

'Psssst!' our leader hisses. 'You're not copying.'

I throw my pompoms into the air.

Beep, beep, beep. Beep. Beep.

I don't look back as I ditch the dancers, sprint to the next station and push in front of the boys lined up to take turns goalkeeping.

'What do you think you're doing?' one of them asks.

I hold up my hand to his face. 'No questions. We're on a tight schedule here.'

I take my place in the goal and wait for the leader to shoot. He kicks before he even realises I'm not supposed to be there.

I barely have to move as I scoop up the ball and kick it back. He's not a very strong kicker. I'd rather the mechanical launcher from school.

Beep, beep, beep. Beep. Beep.

I run to the heading station and take a ball from the bag. The boys are so focused on keeping their balls in the air they don't notice me alongside them.

I start bouncing like a high-powered jack-in-the-box. My forehead is hitting with such precision, you'd think it was made out of metal and the ball was a magnet.

My watch beeps again and I run to the cones.

The group leader is onto me. 'You!' he says. 'Go back to your station!'

I pretend I don't hear and tackle one of the boys for their ball. I start dribbling through the cones, left foot one way and right foot on the way back. I do it again and again, not stopping long enough to give anyone a chance to get the ball away from me.

Beep, beep, beep. Beep. Beep.

Four down, one to go.

I sprint across the home stretch to the southern goal and line up behind the boys to take a shot.

Their leader steps in front of me, trying to block me from shooting. 'This is not your station,' he says. 'Don't make a scene.'

I put my hands on my hips and stand on tiptoes. I'm almost eye-level with him. 'You're the one making a scene,' I say. 'Let me shoot.'

A section of the crowd behind the goal sees the controversy. They start to chant. '*Let her shoot, let her shoot, let her shoot!*'

I squint at the front row. It's the anti-princesses, yelling and waving their arms at the surrounding seats. They must be leading the chant.

Embarrassed, the last group leader steps out of my way. Daniel Hastie's words echo through my head. *'Show us what you got out there, huh?'*

I pick up the ball, turn my back to the goal, bounce the ball on the ground as hard as I can, then throw my body backwards.

The ball reaches head-height and I kick my legs out like the blades of a pair of scissors. With my torso horizontal in mid-air and one

leg extended vertically, my body is positioned almost perfectly at ninety degrees.

I flick out my right boot and it connects with the ball, sending it over my head towards the goal.

I land on the ground with a thump. There's a split second of silence before the stadium erupts. I cover my ears, the applause is so loud.

'You did a bicycle kick!' one boy screams. 'That's an almost impossible manoeuvre!'

'That was amazing!' another squeals.

I shelter my eyes and wave to the crowd. I can just make out Chloe, Bella and Emily hugging and jumping and yelling behind the posts.

Suddenly, the group leader picks me up and puts me on his shoulders. I don't quite understand what's going on until I see the goal.

The ball made it to the dead-centre of the net. A perfect goal.

EPILOGUE

Manchester won the big game but Newcastle came close. I actually found myself cheering for the Jets. There's something extra awesome about seeing the underdogs put up a great fight.

The final score was 4–3, but my family hardly remembers that part. All they've been talking about is my bicycle kick at half-time. Dad wants me to run a special training session with his players so I can teach them how to do it.

I must have impressed the pros too, because after the game my whole family got invited down to the dressing-rooms. Oliver got every player's signature on his cast. He won't ever want to take it off.

Mr Talbot swears it was just a big misunderstanding that I was relegated to the cheer squad. He was extremely apologetic after the whole kerfuffle. Lucky for him that he didn't do it on purpose, otherwise he would have had the anti-princesses to deal with.

Emily's lunchtimes are free again and she's making a mint from her online tutoring. The Anti-Princess Club website is bigger and better than ever. It's also strictly bully-free. A bunch of teachers are pitching in to help in the maths chatroom, but none of them do as good a job as Emily.

Mr Ashton has been sentenced to detention duty for the rest of the term. Mrs O'Neill was thoroughly unimpressed with his rocket and perfume experiments, and told him to stick to the school curriculum rather than being influenced by toy shops. Mrs O'Neill assures Chloe she will be launching many rockets in the future – just as long as they don't smell like rotten eggs.

Bella topped the class with her wedding outfit design. Mr Ashton was speechless when he saw us on television. A tour company is now marketing 'bridge weddings' to the rest of the world and they've asked Bella if they can copy her jumpsuit design. I told her she needs to get her priorities straight – I'm still waiting for my chin-up bar.

Svetlana Karpinskaia and Daniel Hastie's wedding was on the covers of at least eight trashy magazines – including *Pose*. Not that I really care for gossip.

I also don't care for fairytale endings, but at least Svetlana was rescued by the anti-princesses rather than a knight in shining armour. Whatever lies ahead, there's one thing I'm certain of: we won't need rescuing.